Josephine ~~has always~~ always wanted to write. She has created poetry, plays, TV dramas, wildlife stories, thrillers and teenage novels, and retold many of the great classic stories and fairy tales. Her favourite themes are romance, suspense and the supernatural – she loved that sort of book when she was growing up.

She lives with her husband in a very old house in the country. They have six children and five grandchildren, as well as a horse, a pony, a donkey, three dogs, two cats, lots of guineapigs and a goldfish.

R00730

Other titles available from
Hodder Children's Books

Owl Light
Night People
Maggie Pearson

Companions of the Night
Vivian Vande Velde

Look for me by Moonlight
Mary Downing Hahn

Night World series
Lisa J. Smith

Ghost Chamber
Celia Rees

Hauntings
Susan Price

HERO

Josephine Poole

*Hodder
Children's
Books*

a division of Hodder Headline plc

First published in Great Britain in 1997
by Hodder Children's Books

A CIP catalogue record for this title is available
from the British Library

ISBN 0 340 68320 1

Typeset by Palimpsest Book Production Limited,
Polmont, Stirlingshire
Printed and bound in Great Britain by
Cox & Wyman Ltd, Reading, Berks.

Hodder Children's Books
A division of Hodder Headline PLC
338 Euston Road
London NW1 3BH

For Matt, with love and gratitude

The author wishes to thank Jim Brookbank
for his kindness and help.

Chapter One

This is our new house. It is very old and cold and dark, and too big for just two people, my mother and me. It was left to my mother by an old relation called Cousin Alice, a person she knew nothing about until the solicitor's letter arrived like a bomb in our London flat. So – here we are.

Cousin Alice died in a nursing home. At least she didn't die here. Her gloomy furniture still stands in the rooms, which is lucky in a way, because the only thing we had sent from London is the grand piano. That's why my mother wanted to come – so she could get it out of store, and put it in the best place. That's true – you can believe it.

This house is way down in the West Country, where most people wouldn't dream of living. We arrived half an hour ago. I'm sitting in bed writing this. I'm wearing my cap and jacket plus a blanket wrapped round me but I'm still shivering.

I hope our poor cat is all right. He shot off as soon as we opened the car, before I could butter his paws. He's a London cat, so he'll hate it here. I'm a London girl. Mum has promised we'll go back if we can't bear it. I don't think I can.

Here she comes with a mug of hot something – hide this under the duvet.

'Are you dismal, Florry?'

'Yes.'

She sat down on the side of the bed, making it creak. She's six foot tall, and no lightweight. 'Have some cocoa.'

'Has Foss come back?'

'He will. He's exploring. Hunting things in the bushes.'

'Getting chased and killed.'

'Nonsense!' She was looking at me anxiously, tenderly. That's how she gets her own way – because she's so loving. You know all she wants is for you to

2

be happy, so you give in. And you pick up the pieces when her wild ideas don't work.

'This is such a nice room in daylight.'

'Is it?'

'You're worn out! Snuggle down, have a good sleep. Remember, I'm just next door if you want me.' She leant forward and hugged me. 'Goodnight, sweetheart.'

I gave her a grudging kiss. I knew exactly what would happen. Sure enough, she went downstairs with my empty mug, and two minutes later I heard her fingering her precious piano. Soon she was playing so hard that if a burglar got in and I screamed my head off, she wouldn't hear a thing.

Maybe I'll feel better tomorrow.

Tomorrow is Christmas Eve.

The cocoa was good. I took off my jacket, wrapped it round my feet and lay down in bed. I was tired right through to my bones. I shut my eyes and took deep relaxing breaths. After a while my thoughts stopped flicking about and I listened to the noise Mum was making, which was really quite pleasant. I let myself travel on the tune – up, up into the pale blue sky, skimming and wheeling with the birds. Far below lay a neat landscape, little fields and villages and woods with the sea in the distance. At some point I fell asleep and my imagination turned into a dream.

I was still flying, but I wasn't free any more. There were straps round my body, and some sort of a helmet on my head with a wire dangling from it that I noticed out of the corner of my eye. But I couldn't look about, because I had to stare straight ahead. I was anxious in my dream, very anxious. There were people with me, close, but I couldn't look at them. I had to make some sort of a decision for these people – a very important decision.

Mum was thundering now on the piano, making a roaring, thumping din not musical at all. There was a red glow on my right that moved with me, somehow part of my flight. It was getting bigger and brighter. My heart began to beat so hard, I could scarcely breathe. I had to make this decision – I had to do something about these people.

4

Then one by one they dropped away, as if they had been swallowed up. But my heart was still pounding. The red glow hadn't gone. It was much bigger now – it was spreading fast – separating into flames—

The friendly landscape far below had turned into the sea. The sea was getting closer very quickly, it was grey and wrinkled like dead skin. Now I was hurtling at it – it was rising to get me – a deafening roar filled my ears so I couldn't hear my own screams—

I woke up, sweating all over. My room was dark, the house was silent. I lay for a minute getting my bearings, letting out the panic. Oh God what a dream!

I sat up and wiped my clammy face. Then I got out of bed and padded barefoot into Mum's room next door. She hadn't drawn her curtains and the moon shone full across the floor, onto her clothes tumbled over a chair. She was lying on her back, and her hair, which is long and red and very beautiful, surrounded her sleeping face like a grey shadow.

It was a double bed. I lifted the side of the duvet and crept in. I was careful not to touch her, but after a while her comforting warmth took over and I slept.

Chapter Two

I could hear Mum singing outside when I woke up, and I went to the window and looked down. She was just below in her fur hat and old leather coat, unloading the car. It was a beautiful day. I knocked on the pane. She looked up and shouted, 'Put on your jacket if you're coming out here! It's freezing!'

I went into my room and dressed. I didn't agree with Mum that it was nice in daylight. It had the usual furniture – bed, chest of drawers, wardrobe, one chair – but it didn't have a rug or a lampshade, and the only ornament was a red and white china spaniel on the mantelpiece. I called it a bare room, but when I'd arranged my things it would look better. I ran downstairs. The front door was open and an icy draught whistled through the house.

We'd arrived after dark, so I hadn't seen the garden. It was large and untidy, full of bushes and grim bony trees – you couldn't imagine they would ever have leaves. The grass was rough and yellow, stiff with frost, with a track across it where we'd driven to the front door. The square old house looked plain and rather dilapidated. Its plaster had peeled off in patches, and all the creeping things that grew up the walls had muddled into each other like tangled hair, through which the windows peered anxiously.

I unstrapped the Christmas tree from the roof rack and carried it in. It was a real one, with roots in a plastic bag full of soil. The bag burst as I put it down, so I had to find a pot for it. There was a big one on a stand by the stairs, blue with a dragon pattern. The tree fitted in nicely. I scooped up the earth and put it round the roots, and then I found a jug in the kitchen, and watered it. By the time I'd saved its life, Mum had finished unloading and the front door was shut, and our square tiled hall looked like an airport departure lounge during a strike.

After that we had breakfast. I was terribly worried about our cat.

'Has Foss showed up?'

'Not yet, but he will.'

But I knew I would find him mangled under a bush, and I wanted to cry.

Mum said, 'I'm going to the village, for milk and eggs and some bread. Fresh country bread! You've never tasted proper bread!'

'I'll stay here. I want to sort out my stuff.'

'All right. I won't be long. Lock me out, and don't answer the door.'

She reversed across the garden in jerks, polluting the air with clouds of exhaust, and after a brief encounter with the gatepost, turned backwards into the lane. I stayed outside for a while, calling Foss, and searching for his corpse under the bushes. It was terribly cold, and he wasn't there, and he didn't come. The remains of a swing hung from one of the trees. I imagined old Cousin Alice as a child in a bonnet and skirts, kicking herself high into the branches. I thought, We could make this into a lovely garden. If we stayed, I thought. *But we're not staying*. Okay, for Christmas, but after that I won't. No houses, no neighbours, no friends: Mum's got her piano but what is there here for me? Nothing!

I went in and heaved my things upstairs to my room. I unrolled my posters and put them up. There was a picture already hanging over the mantelpiece, a black-and-white photo of an aeroplane with some blokes standing grinning beside it. I didn't examine it closely but there was plenty of wall space, so I didn't bother to take it down. I was admiring my room, which did look more cheerful, when I heard something scrabbling overhead. My heart skipped a beat – then I thought, Foss! I ran out onto the landing and called him. No answer – not a sound.

Mum had said there was an attic. I went down the passage, which was narrow and dark, and there were stairs at the end. I went up, calling, 'Foss, Foss!' I can't deny that my heart was beating extremely. It was partly the spiders – I hate spiders. I didn't see any, but there were a lot of cobwebs. Nobody had been up here for a long, long time.

The stairs ended at a door. It wasn't properly shut – Foss must have pushed his way in, and it must have swung to behind him. I opened it with my heart in my mouth – and out he shot with a yowl of rage, his fur on end and his tail like a brush.

But I was spellbound by the attic. It took up all the roof space, so it was huge, and freezing cold. It had no windows, but several of the slates had slipped so light came through. It was crammed with trunks and boxes and bundles of newspapers; as my eyes adjusted to the gloom I saw more and more things, broken chairs and clocks and mirrors and china, heaps of dusty blankets and old curtains. For hundreds of years, anything that needed mending or storing in this house had been hauled up here, and forgotten. Treasures – secrets—

There was a trunk near me which had been padlocked, but the screws had broken. I lifted the lid. It was full of old clothes. On top lay a blue peaked cap, very faded and

11

stained, with a black band round it and a badge at the front. I took it out to see what was on the badge, but the light wasn't good enough. I climbed over a sofa and found an old dolls' pram, and a little horse on wheels. I found a dressmaker's dummy with bits of cream satin still pinned on it – a wedding that never happened? Secrets. I caught sight of my own face distorted in a cracked mirror – like a goblin, all eyes and curly black hair. When I looked up, I saw a young man in the corner, watching me.

My heart gave a lurch. *Mum told me to lock the door and I forgot*. I stepped back hastily and the mirror toppled but saved itself on a chair. No way could I get out of the attic before he grabbed me. But he didn't move. So then I looked at him properly. He was standing in the darkest corner and his clothes merged into the shadows, so I couldn't see him clearly, apart from his face. It was a nice face. He had dark hair cut short, dark eyes and a straight nose. He was smiling at me and there was nothing wrong with that – it was a natural, friendly smile.

He said, 'I'm sorry I frightened you. It's quite all right, I'm not a burglar. I used to live here.' His voice was friendly, as if we already knew each other. He nodded at the cap I still had in my hand, and said, 'I used to wear that.'

I imagined him coming up here, opening the trunk, trying on the old cap. It couldn't have been so very long ago – he didn't look more than twenty.

'I'm Bo,' he said.

What sort of a name was that? He pronounced it like 'Bo' in Bo-Peep.

'I'm Florence.'

'Hallo.'

'Hi.'

'So you've just moved in,' he said.

'Last night. You may have heard of my mother, Marie Dangerfield? She used to be a singer.'

'I haven't, I'm afraid.'

'She still plays the piano and writes music. What are you doing up here?'

'I've been waiting for you.'

'For me? Why?'

'Because I need your help.'

13

Now here I was having a conversation with a complete stranger, something I'd been forbidden to do and never did. So I should explain how it happened. Bo was not like other people. I knew instantly that he was someone I could trust, he was a person who had never done a mean or a cruel thing. I knew it without any doubt whatever. Bo was a *shining* person. I can't put it any other way.

'*My* help? What sort of help?'

He came closer. He knew his way in the attic, he didn't have to scramble over the jumble of things. He wore a light blue shirt, open at the neck with the sleeves rolled up, and a loosely knotted plain black tie. His trousers were dullish blue – not jeans. I could see that although his eyebrows were so dark, they didn't meet in the middle, and his eyes had cheerful hazel lights. His mouth had lines at the corners as if he laughed a lot. But now he wasn't being funny.

'Something has disappeared from the house, something that belongs here.'

'Something of yours?'

'Yes. Yes, it's mine, in a way. But really it's more of a family thing—'

'Like an heirloom?'

He hesitated, then he said, 'That would be one way of describing it.'

'Why can't you get it back yourself?'

'I would if I could,' he said.

There was something so sad in the way he spoke, it twisted my heart.

He said, 'You see I'm not free, I can't go into all the places where you can go.'

'You mean people would recognise you, but I'm not known round here. Okay. Do you know who took it?'

'I think so.'

'Is it going to be dangerous? Because Mum won't have it, if so.'

'It isn't worth a great deal of money. It's a question of who has the right to it. Do you know what I mean?'

I shrugged and made a face, the way I do when I don't understand. I said, 'You'd better tell me what it looks like.'

'It's in a box, a flat black box, about six inches by three.'

'What size is that?'

He smiled, and showed me with his hands.

'A sort of jewellery box,' I said. Suddenly I heard Mum calling me, far below.

'I'll have to go.' I didn't want her up here. She was going to be cross with me anyway for not locking the door. I started scrambling over the furniture.

'Florence – the box is very important – to me at least,' he said. 'Remember, if you want me, you can always get me up here. If you hold the cap, I'll come—'

I turned my head, stared back at him. 'You mean, like a radio signal?'

He really laughed then, as if I'd meant to make a joke. 'That's it – exactly!'

'Okay. 'Bye.'

Mum was in the kitchen, putting away the shopping.

'Foss is back,' I told her, out of breath.

'Oh Florry, you never locked the door. I wish you'd be more careful! Anyone could have got in!'

'I'm sorry, Mum.'

I did mean to tell her about Bo, partly because I knew how much she'd like him.

But she was upset, and if I said I'd been talking to an unknown man in the attic, there'd be a truly mega row. So I put it off for the moment. They were sure to meet soon, so I wasn't being deceitful, I was saving her unnecessary worry. I was also chickening out. My mother is hardly ever angry, but she used to sing opera, and opera is what you get when she is.

I checked the attic after lunch, but Bo had gone. He must have let himself out by the front door while we were in the kitchen. That afternoon we decorated the tree, and then we lit the fire in the library, the room where Mum had her piano. She scribbled and played, she was inspired I could tell by the crumpled manuscript paper lying around her. I sat on the floor by the fire with Foss on my lap.

You don't notice winter darkness so much in London, with all the lights and the people. Here in the depths of the country, it was like being out at sea. If we needed the neighbours, there weren't any. If we weren't talking, if Mum wasn't playing, there was silence. And how soon the shadows crept forward from their corners, began to engulf the room!

The sun was far down now, its red ball poised on the hill. The sky was luminous, softly darkening round the pinprick of a solitary star. A bird called, just a few rapid notes across the garden. As the light faded, the bushes seemed to thicken and brace themselves against the frost. The frost was like breath against the tall french windows.

'Carols?' said Mum into the silence.

'Carols?'

'You know we always sing carols on Christmas Eve!'

So she played and we sang. Then such a weird feeling grew on me, that we were not alone. There were invisible listeners in the rooms in this old house – shadowy forms just outside in the hall, on the stairs – I knew they were there.

We sang all our favourites, and then she taught me a new one, and we sang that. And she sang because she loves to; but soon I accepted the listeners, and I sang for them. Poor ghosts – I sang for them with all my heart.

18

'Oh Florry, what a beautiful voice you have got,' said my mother as she got up from the piano. End of subject, I didn't even look at her. One performer in a family is enough.

It was black dark now, and I pulled the curtains shut.

This was the strangest Christmas Eve I had ever known.

Chapter Three

On Christmas morning the three of us always open our stockings in Mum's bed – at least, Foss has a paper bag because he can't manage a stocking. This year I had found him a clockwork spider, as well as several cattish treats. The spider hopped and squeaked, and he didn't like it at all. Mum's had the usual comb/soap/hand cream/bath essence/barley sugar which she eats a lot of, plus a tape, the recording she wanted. Mine was all surprises and very good. We had a tray of tea and biscuits upstairs, and were extremely happy and comfortable, and if Foss got tiresome we kept him off with the spider.

After we dressed, I peeled sprouts and potatoes while Mum put the ready-stuffed turkey into the oven, and the Christmas pudding to boil on top. Then we heaped on our thickest outdoor clothes and went off to find a church. I thought we'd take the car, but she wanted to walk. It was another sparkling clear, freezing day, and according to her, it wasn't far to the village. So we crunched across our frosty grass and through our rickety gate.

'Which way?'

'Right.' She strode down the lane, I had to trot to keep up. The hedges were tall on both sides but she could see over the top of them.

'Why don't you do up your coat?'

'I'm not *cold*, Florry! This walk is just doing me so much good.' She began taking deep breaths. 'It's like doses of salts clearing out my poor tubes.'

By 'tubes' she meant her breathing organs, which are weak, and the reason why she stopped singing opera soon after I was born.

'But I wish you would do it up.'

'Oh, Florry! Don't *fuss*! I said, I'm not cold!'

I was. I wondered how long it took to

get frostbite. I had my scarf up over my face, because the freezing air burnt the inside of my nose. We passed a garden gate with a doctor's nameplate on it. I made a mental note of it, hoping it wouldn't be necessary.

It seemed like fifty miles to Great Wenham, but we reached it at last. It wasn't a picture-postcard village. The cottage roofs were mostly slate, the streets were narrow, the shops were small and dark. We came into a square and there in front of us was the ancient church, surrounded by yew trees and gravestones. People were coming out, but Mum never minds missing a service – in fact she only goes to one by accident. We waited politely by the gate. The villagers were not ashamed of scrutinising us quite openly. Some of them said, 'Good morning,' but Mum was looking over their heads with her fixed smile. I saw that she seemed rude – how could they know that she was working out a tune in her head? I mumbled, 'Good morning,' and felt my face turn scarlet. I wished I wasn't so tall and thin. My clothes always look wrong – either they've just been bought with room for growth, or I've already grown out of them. And my hair has a wild life of its own.

When the villagers had gone, Mum went into the church, but I stayed outside in the graveyard. Now I was the only person about, not counting a stout dog – a red and white spaniel, the sort I like with a friendly face. He was standing under a yew tree, looking at me – as if he was waiting for me. So I said, 'Hallo, Dog, you look exactly like the china dog on my mantelpiece,' which he did. I don't usually talk aloud to dogs, but he was on his own and so was I. But he ignored my outstretched hand, and trotted off between the graves. So I followed. I had nothing else to do.

Soon we came to the far end of the churchyard, where no-one had cut the grass, and there were no graves to leave Christmas flowers on. Beyond the wall, small fields with hedges round them led up to a wood, and above was the beautifully blue sky. I thought, I could learn to ride. It would be wonderful to gallop up there and go into that wood. I spotted a bird, high above, just hanging on wide wings – that's to say it looked like a speck from where I was, but I knew it must be huge. As I watched, it let out a wild, fierce cry.

But suddenly I noticed what Dog was doing. There was just one cross out here on its own. He was scrabbling away in front of it as if he meant to get to the dead person inside.

'Stop it!' I shouted. 'Stop it at once! You can't do that!' But he took no notice at all. So I dashed up to him, waving my arms, and he ran away then. In fact he hadn't done any harm – the grass here was still white with frost, the earth as hard as iron. He hadn't made a mark. I read the inscription on the cross:

BEAUMONT VESEY DFC
1923–1943
REMEMBERED WITH PRIDE

That was all it said. Very plain, very sad.

Mum was waving from the church. I got up and ran across to join her, and we set off briskly for home. We passed a café in the square called Marchant's Tea Shoppe. It would have been good to go in for coffee, but there were two placards in the window: one said SOLD and the other, CLOSED. I could see Marchant among the dark little tables and chairs and arrangements of everlasting flowers. He wore brown slacks and a beige hand-knitted cardigan; he was balding with a droopy grey moustache and a sour expression. I disliked him immediately.

'What's DFC?' I asked Mum as we walked down the lane.

'Distinguished Flying Cross. Why?'

'I saw it on a cross in the churchyard.'

After a while we met Foss coming down the lane, looking for us, and we all went into the house together. As soon as we opened the door, the Christmas smell gushed out – roast turkey and plum pudding. It didn't take long to cook the vegetables, and the kitchen table looked festive with the napkins and bottle of alcohol-free wine we had brought from London. We ate till we could eat no more.

Then Mum went into the library to try out the music in her head, while I switched on the kettle and stacked the dirty things in the sink. We never wash up on Christmas Day. I stuffed myself with chocolates, feeling full and happy, sort of listening to the noise Mum was making, as well as the kettle starting to sing. I made the coffee and carried it in – and there was Bo outside in the garden, leaning against the window frame, listening to Mum doodling on the keys. But she was sitting with her back to the glass, so of course she hadn't seen him.

I put down the mugs and went to the french windows, but the safety key was stiff and I had a job to unlock it. And at last Mum noticed me and said in surprise, 'My darling love, why, in Heaven's name, are you trying to open the window?'

Then I saw that Bo had gone.

I ran out of the room and across the hall and looked out of the front door. There was nobody in the garden. He'd seen that Mum was busy and he hadn't wanted to intrude. It was bitterly cold outside, and he'd been still in his shirtsleeves. I was sorry he'd gone. It would have been an excellent chance for Mum to meet him.

When I got back to the library, she opened her mouth to speak, but instead she began to cough. By the time that was over, all she could do was look at me apologetically and say, 'Only a raisin, Florry. I ate too much pudding.' But we both knew it wasn't true.

Last time she'd been ill, she'd had to go to hospital. The worry of it clouded the rest of Christmas Day. Mum made herself extra bright and cheerful, and we kept the fire going and the hot drinks coming. But it wasn't any use. As soon as we went to bed, her cough came back in earnest – that regular dusty cough I knew too well, that kept me awake waiting for the next one. Soon I couldn't bear it and I knocked on her door and went in.

'Will you drink something hot if I bring it?'

'No, sweetheart, really – go back to bed. I've got some water. I'll be fine in a minute.'

'You don't sound fine. What would you like? Tea?'

'Well – It would be so nice, if you really don't mind—'

I went down and made tea. The sink was

full of the Christmas pans and glasses and plates, and Mum would have to stay in bed tomorrow. I laid a tray. In the hall the cold seemed to wrap round me like an icy scarf, and then I saw that the dining-room door was open. I put down the tray on the stairs and went to shut it. I put out my hand to the door – and then I saw.

The fireplace was opposite the doorway, with a mirror hanging above. In the glass was reflected a shadowy face. It should have been mine. It wasn't.

I couldn't move, I couldn't breathe. I could only stare. The reflection was sharpening – dark eyes, a smile – a face I knew.

Why was Bo in the glass, instead of me? Was he standing just behind me? I spun round, but the hall was empty. So was the mirror when I peered cautiously at it once more. Quite empty, apart from the specks and smudges you get in old glass.

I had to use both hands to shut the door because they were trembling so. I picked up the tray and carried it to Mum with the mug and jug and teapot jittering all the way. I poured out sloppily and sat on the side of the bed.

'You're shaking,' she whispered, observing me over the mug. 'It's not cold in here, is it? I put the heater on.'

'It's freezing downstairs.'

She reached out a hand and I held it in mine. After a while I said, 'Do you think it's possible – possible to – to *see* someone, when they aren't really there?'

'Like ghosts, do you mean?'

'No, not ghosts. Say you met someone and you'd been thinking about them and you wanted to know them better. And then you thought you saw – you seemed to see their face.'

'If you were an imaginative sort of person, and it was late and you were tired and the light wasn't good – yes, I should think you—' cough, cough— 'I should think you might. Why? Who've you been seeing?' I wasn't looking at her but I knew she was anxiously scanning my face. 'Is it Dad?'

She's always afraid I miss him. I might, if he missed me.

'No, not him! Nothing to do with him.'

'Who then?'

'Nobody special. I just wondered. Have you taken your tubes prescription?'

'I left it in London.'

'Idiot!'

'I know. Sorry, Florry!' she said in the tiny voice that was meant to make me laugh, but made her cough instead.

When I went to my room I stood by the window for a minute, looking out. It was a lovely night. I know a few of the constellations but I couldn't find them among the quantities of stars pressed like diamond dust against black velvet. Then something caught my eye and I looked down into the garden. Dog – the spaniel – was sitting on our grass, staring straight up at me. He wasn't panting, or grinning or wagging his tail. He was simply sitting there, staring. I don't know how long he stayed.

Luckily Foss hadn't seen him. *He* was lying on my bed, very comfortable. When I got in I took him with me, clasped in my arms for warmth, but he didn't mind. He's good like that.

Chapter Four

I didn't wake next morning till after ten. I didn't go in to Mum because all was quiet and I hoped she was still sleeping. But when I went down to the kitchen there she was, propped against the cooker in her nightgown and shawl, looking awful.

'I meant to do the washing up,' she croaked.

'You go straight back to bed. I'll get the doctor.'

'Darling you can't. It's Boxing Day. There won't be one.'

I guided her upstairs, tidied the bed round her, arranged the pillows. In a few minutes the room looked neat, and I dusted round quickly with a sock. Then I grabbed my boots and jacket, and ran down the garden and up the lane. I was only just in time because the gate I had noticed, with Dr Lawson's name on it, was open and his car was nosing out. I was so desperate, I stood in front of it, waving my arms, so that he had to stop. He opened his door and looked out.

'It's an emergency!' I shouted. 'My mother's terribly ill and you must come and look at her at once, now, please!'

'Where is she?'

'Next door – that's to say up the road, on the left, and I don't know what the house is called, we only moved in two nights ago.'

'I know where you mean. Hop in.'

I hopped, and we shot away. I said, 'She's got a prescription but she left it in London.' I was still getting my breath from running.

'What's it for, do you know?'

'Not exactly. It's her tubes.' That sounded vague so I added, 'Her breath. Her lungs.'

We'd already reached our place and he hauled the car round, scorched up the garden and jammed on the brakes by the house. We both jumped out and went in by the back.

'Where is she? In Miss Vesey's room?' He was already on the stairs.

I knew that name from somewhere but I didn't stop to think about it. 'The first door at the top.'

I followed him, and noticed how the urgency of the call suddenly vanished, how calmly and quietly he pushed the door open and went in.

She was asleep, her face as white as the pillows. Her nightdress, the Victorian sort with lace and long sleeves, was also white, and the whole effect was deathly. Only her long red wavy hair, spread out to below her shoulders, gave colour to that bed.

Dr Lawson said in a low voice, 'You didn't tell me her name.'

'Marie. Marie Dangerfield.'

He sat down on the side of the bed. 'Mrs Dangerfield?'

She opened her eyes and looked at him. Her eyes are deep blue, and the fact that she can't see much without her specs does not affect the beauty of them. She looked at him as if she'd woken up into a different world.

I closed the door and went downstairs. I put the kettle on, removed Foss from a saucepan where he was scoffing the last of the Christmas gravy, and set to work on the washing up. After a while I heard Dr Lawson on the stairs, and he called, 'Florence?'

'In the kitchen.' He came in. 'Would you like some coffee?'

'Thanks.' He looked slightly dazed.

'Is she really ill? Please sit down.' I moved Foss and the teatowel he was squatting on, from the only available chair.

'It's a good thing you fetched me. She's got a touch of pleurisy, and that's extremely painful, but it shouldn't last long. I've given her some antibiotics. Take her hot drinks, and keep her in bed. Thanks,' he said as I put his coffee and the milk and sugar on the table. 'I wish I had a nice useful daughter.'

'You mean you haven't got one?' It was too much to hope that he had a girl of my age. 'Or is she nasty and useless?' Then I blushed because that sounded stupid and even rude. But he only laughed.

'I haven't got any children at all. I'm afraid I'm just a cross old bachelor.'

He didn't look cross. He wasn't handsome, but he looked kind and smiling and countrified, with the sort of red face that is used to being out in all weathers. He wasn't old, either – not much older than Mum. It suddenly struck me that he would make an excellent friend for her. It was his size that put this into my head, because he was huge – tall and heavy, though not fat. The kitchen chair creaked whenever he moved. So I said without thinking, 'Are you musical?' If he wasn't, that was the end. No one who wasn't could bear it.

'Very much so,' he replied. 'When you said Marie Dangerfield, I couldn't believe it was the same person. But she hasn't changed much since I saw her on stage – it must be fifteen years ago. I'm still in a state of shock,' and he pushed the fingers of both hands through his hair, so that it stood on end, and I had to look away not to laugh.

He emptied his mug in one swig, stood up and said, 'I must go. Could you ask your father to be sure to collect this prescription from Barnstaple this evening? The chemist opens at six,' and he put a piece of scrawled paper on the table. 'What's the matter?' he said, looking at me with his kind little eyes.

'Just my father doesn't live with us any more. They're divorced.' I could feel my face turning bright red.

'I'm so sorry,' he said. 'In that case I'll fetch it myself and come back this evening. Don't worry, I'd have looked in anyway to see how she's getting on. Don't let her forget to take her pills.' He patted my shoulder and left. I waved from the back door, but he was too busy reversing to notice.

When I looked into the fridge and cupboards I saw that we had hardly any food left. I made a soup from the turkey bones and the rest of the stuffing and bread sauce. It didn't look very nice so I stirred in some cranberry jelly, and took a bowl of it to Mum. She struggled up in bed and I put the tray on her lap.

'Soup made by me,' I said. 'Guess what's in it.'

She did.

'Lovely, darling,' she said, gallantly finishing the bowlful under my stern gaze. 'Really warming and nourishing.' I gave her the pills Dr Lawson had left. As I was going out, she called after me, 'Will you play to me this afternoon? It would be such a treat. Leave the door open so I can hear properly.'

I knew that for her the piano is a living creature that needs to speak, and anyone playing is better for it than silence. She was quite capable of tottering downstairs to please it, if I didn't. She is quite mad in some ways, my mother. I said angrily, 'I wish you played something portable.'

'Why?'

'You could have it in your bedroom and not bother me.'

'Oh Florry – if it's a bother—'

'No, no, I will, I will.'

I didn't fancy my soup, so I went straight to the library. I turned the heater to max, opened the piano and sat down. I don't play well, I don't want to play well, and I hadn't brought any music with me. But Mum takes Bach's *Anna Magdalena* with her everywhere, so I played through the book, and then I played some things I knew by heart. I was into *Für Elise*, jazzing it up and making it sound really silly, I was giggling to myself, when the library turned suddenly cold. It was suddenly as cold as a tomb, though the heater beside me was still working full blast.

My body temperature started to drop, and I stopped messing about. I was sure that there was somebody else in the room. The lid of the piano was up and blocked part of my view. 'Mum?' I said. I didn't think it was her. But there had to be – someone – just behind the piano. Had I remembered to lock the back door? Probably not. I began to shiver all over, not only with cold. Not knowing was worse than anything – I slammed my hands down on the keys and stood up.

It was Bo. I was so relieved, I sat down again hard on the stool.

'You just gave me the most horrible fright.' I shut the piano.

'I'm truly sorry,' he said. I saw that he was. 'I couldn't help it.'

'It's not your fault. I was making such a racket, I didn't hear you come in.' He was still standing there as if he didn't quite know what to do or say to put things right. I went on, 'I haven't forgotten about your box, but Mum's ill, I had to get the doctor. He's coming again tonight. I'm sorry it's so cold in here. Don't you ever wear a sweater?'

'I'm used to it.' Then he added, 'It always was a cold house.'

'Let's go into the kitchen. Would you like some coffee?'

'No, thanks – not for me.'

The kitchen end of the house was almost dark, away from the setting sun. His clothes seemed to melt into the gloom of the cupboards; only his face showed clearly. It reminded me of how I'd imagined him in the mirror. I put out my hand to the light switch. He said at once, 'No, don't turn the light on.' I stared at him. He said, 'It's easier for me like this. I've been thinking, if you knew more about me, it would be helpful.'

'Okay, that's a good idea.' I filled the kettle, plugged it in, put coffee in mugs for Mum and me, got out the milk and sugar. All the time I was waiting to hear what he had to say. But he said no more.

'What sort of job do you do?' I asked at last.

'I haven't got a job.'

That surprised me, because he had very much the look of a person who had a pretty demanding job. But I repeated what I'd heard Mum say to people in his position, 'I expect you'll soon have some luck.'

'My luck ran out,' he said.

He didn't sound despairing about it – he was simply stating a fact. I made the coffee. I said, 'I'll just take this mug up to Mum, and I'll be right back. Don't go, will you?'

I turned with Mum's coffee in my hand – and there she was, in the kitchen doorway. She looked as white as a ghost. She turned on the light. 'Florry—' Her voice sounded strange – as if she wasn't sure who I was.

'I've just made you some coffee.'

'I heard you talking, I wondered who was here. Florry. Who were you talking to?'

I looked round, to introduce Bo.

Bo had gone. Not through the back door

because I was standing in front of it. Not into the passage where Mum was staring at me as if I was crazy. There was no other natural way of leaving the kitchen, apart from the window which was shut.

Bo had vanished.

Chapter Five

'You were talking to someone.'

'I was talking to myself.'

'You're so pale, Florry. What's been happening?'

'Nothing, Mum! I just got a fright when you suddenly appeared downstairs. You look terrible. Dr Lawson said you had to stay in bed, and he'll blame me.' Then I had to sit because my legs were so shaky. Mum put her hand on my forehead in case I had a fever, but it was cold.

She said, 'I wish you'd tell me the truth.'

'I am! I was talking to someone who doesn't exist. That is honestly the truth. Don't worry about it!'

At last she went upstairs.

I poured the cold coffee down the sink. There weren't any curtains in the kitchen.

At any moment I might see Bo through the glass. At any moment he might materialise behind me. I was very, very scared.

But then I began to despise myself. I liked him a lot, and he hadn't changed – what was I doing, letting in all this panic? I remembered how he'd looked in the library – it must be horrible not to be able to come back without frightening people.

I hadn't eaten anything much all day. I made myself a sandwich with the last of the bread, I put it on a plate and sat down and ate it. I did this slowly and deliberately with the idea of calming myself. Then I said, 'Bo,' in a low voice. But he wasn't to be summoned like a dog. He didn't come, he thought I'd given him up. He couldn't hope for help from me any more.

I was still sitting miserably at the table, when there was a bang on the door and it opened with a snap. I jumped so I nearly fell off the chair. It was Dr Lawson, carrying a paper bag and a bulky brown envelope. 'Sorry to startle you,' he said cheerfully, and then he saw how gloomy I looked.

'My dear Florence, what's the matter? Is it your mother? Is she worse?'

He spoke so kindly, I felt the stupid tears prickling my eyelids. I suddenly wanted to tell him about Bo – *I've seen a ghost – he needs my help but he's gone and I can't get him back* – Instead I said, 'No, she's fine,' in the tight voice you get when you're trying not to cry.

'Then there's no need for you to worry. I'll go up and see her and then I'll come back and report. I won't be a minute.'

But he took much longer than that. I had time to tidy the kitchen, I even swept the floor. I found the rest of the wine and put it on the table, with a glass. When he came back I could see that his report was good. 'I looked out some old programmes and press cuttings,' he said. 'She's enjoying them. Thanks,' as I poured out some wine. He lowered himself onto the rickety kitchen chair. 'Cheers. Good health to all.' He drank half his glass at a gulp. 'What is this stuff?'

'It's okay, it hasn't got any alcohol in it.'

'Ah. Well, I'm off duty anyhow. I tell you

what,' he said, looking across at me. 'You must come round and see the puppies. My old Duchess has just had a litter, and she's a bit protective at first. But soon – next week some time – she won't mind a bit. She's a red and white spaniel, lovely temperament. I'll give you one if you like.'

'I'd love one. That's really nice of you.' But then I remembered Foss. 'We've got a cat,' I said.

'So have I. They get on all right – share the same bed.'

'But what about when we go back to London?'

'Why, are you going back?'

Suddenly it struck me that I hadn't thought about London, or missed it at all.

'I don't know,' I said. But he seemed downcast at the thought, so I added, 'I think I've seen your dog.'

'Not Duchess – she's been housebound for a week. There are lots of spaniels her colour round here, though. Long ago there must have been a gallant dog who fathered a great many litters – no thanks, I won't,' as I offered more wine. He stared at the organic dregs in his glass. Presently he said, 'Your mother's afraid this old house is getting you down.'

I should have expected her to talk to him about me. 'No, not at all. I like it.'

'Well, she'll soon be up and about. Great Wenham is a nice village, the people are very friendly. You'll be drawn in. Especially when your family's been here so long.'

'Cousin Alice, you mean. I don't think of her as family. She wasn't called Dangerfield. I don't even know what she was called.'

'Alice Vesey,' he said. 'That was her name. Well, I must go, my clever old dog can open the fridge, so I mustn't be late with her supper. I'll look in again tomorrow to check on our patient but I'm sure she'll be fine. You've got my number, haven't you, in case you need anything?'

We found it in Cousin Alice's old green book, which still lay beside the telephone in the hall.

'Goodnight, then, Florence. Mind you get an early night.'

'I'll go up now.'

'Good girl.'

I took a tray of tea upstairs. The programmes and press cuttings were all over the bed and Mum looked cheerful. It did her good to see how famous she'd been. We read some of them aloud in pompous voices, and drank all the tea. I kissed her goodnight.

The moon was so bright in my room, I didn't need to switch on the light. The first thing I saw was Foss on the sill, staring out of the window. He growled, and as I watched he rose up on his toes. It was spooky seeing him come on the alert, without knowing why. I went to the window with my heart beating fast, I hoped I was going to see Bo down there.

But it was only Dog. He had taken up his position on our grass, and he was staring up, and Foss with frantic yellow eyes glared down. And as I looked at Dog, something Bo had said in the attic suddenly came into my mind. Maybe it wouldn't work, maybe he'd gone for good. But I had to try.

I found my torch and very quietly opened my bedroom door. Mum's door was shut but I could see a line of light under it. I left mine ajar for Foss, I didn't want Mum barging in to let him out, and wondering where I was. I crept across the landing and along the passage to the attic stairs. I didn't turn on any lights. I began creeping up the stairs. Having to be quiet made it worse. My heart was beating loudly enough to wake the house. All those Christmas listeners – as I advanced on their secrets and treasures, they thronged the stairs, mouthing questions about me. The air got so thick I could hardly breathe. I said in my head, I'm going to Bo. I said it again and again.

When I reached the top of the stairs I switched on my torch and opened the door. This was the part I'd been dreading – the jumbled darkness of the furniture and all the personal things – and the very first I happened to spot with the torch was the dressmaker's dummy which did look exactly like a headless body. I screamed aloud and dropped the torch, but luckily it stayed on. I picked it up and waited breathlessly for Mum to come pounding up the stairs. But she didn't, she hadn't heard.

I opened the chest, and there was the cap. Then something inside me said, You're mad. What on earth are you doing? Leave it, go back to bed. You imagined the whole thing. Besides, it said, what if Bo doesn't come? What if it's *somebody else*?

I said in my head, He will come. I lifted out the cap. As I held it, with the torch in my other hand, I examined the badge above the peak. It had wings embroidered on it, with the letters RAF. Then I noticed a name-tape stitched inside. The name on the tape was Beaumont Vesey. At once I remembered the cross in the graveyard.

Bo had died in the Second World War. I looked up, and there he was.

I said, 'This was yours.'

'I did tell you that.'

'I didn't understand what you meant.'

'It was picked up by a fisherman. He sent it back to my sister.'

'Was Alice Vesey your sister?'

'Yes.'

I wanted to ask why his cap had been picked up by a fisherman, when he was in the Royal Air Force, but I didn't like to.

Instead I said, 'I suppose you came back a lot while she was here.'

'No, not at all!' he said, surprised. 'People only come back for a reason. Mine was the box disappearing when my sister left the house. When it comes back – if it ever does – I shall be free to go.'

He sounded as if that would be the most desirable thing in the world.

'You mean you don't *like* coming back?'

'Of course not! Why should I? It's like – like being in leg irons. Please don't think I'm not happy to be here talking to you,' he added quickly. 'It's just that – oh Florence, if you do manage to find it and bring it back, I shall be for ever grateful.' He meant that, he wasn't exaggerating.

'I'll do my best, I really will.' I meant that, too.

My torch battery was beginning to fade. It couldn't compete with the centuries of darkness gathered in the attic. Bo was standing quite close, but he was only a shadowy form, apart from his face. I was glad we were related. He had the nicest possible face. He was a person you could be silent with, and still feel perfectly comfortable.

'I can make myself brighter if you like,' he said.

'That would be good.'

Under my gaze he became clearer, brighter, until he looked like an angel. That sounds crazy – an angel in clothes. But that was what he looked like.

'What did you fly in?'

'A Wellington. A Wellington bomber.'

'It must have been really exciting.'

'You could call it that,' he said.

He said, 'You remember I told you I thought I knew who took the box. There's one person who would have died for it, a man called Roly Marchant. He was my co-pilot. He wanted to take over when we got into trouble, but I made him bale out with the others. Apart from anything else, he was engaged to be married to my sister.'

'But Cousin Alice never married.'

'He was difficult. He had ideas about glory, and he thought he could land the plane. Nobody could have done it. We'd all have been killed.'

'Was he a burgling sort?'

'You mean, did he break in here and steal the box? No, he'd never have done that. Besides, I'd know if he had.'

'There's a Marchant in the village!' I suddenly exclaimed. 'He's got a café. But that could be just a coincidence.'

'It may not be.'

'But the café's been sold!' I cried out, remembering.

'That makes sense. He's got the box, and he's going home. He came from up north somewhere. I think you ought to move fast.'

'I'll go in there tomorrow.'

'Alice would never have given it to him. She'd never have lost it, either – it was her most precious possession. She'd have kept it to the last—'

As I opened my mouth to ask what was in the box, he added, 'There's a picture in my room—'

Then to my dismay I saw that the substance of Bo was changing. He was still bright, but his brightness had started to shimmer as if he consisted only of light. I was afraid he was on the point of going away. The thought was suddenly unbearable.

'Please don't go,' I said.

'I must. I only wish there was more I could do to help. But you're clever and kind and brave. If anyone can find it, you will. I'd have been proud to have someone like you in my crew.'

No one had ever spoken to me like that. I knew Mum thought I was wonderful, but she'd never made a statement of it. But alas, from Bo it sounded somehow final – almost like goodbye.

He was all over bright and shimmering. As I looked at him, he saluted me. Then I knew that I would never see him again. Then I started to cry.

'Please don't go!' I cried out again in despair.

But he vanished.

Chapter Six

I went to bed, but I couldn't sleep. At first I was too sad to think of anything but Bo. He was the most marvellous person I had ever known. If he really had gone, I felt I couldn't bear the loss.

But after a while I began remembering all the things he'd said. I thought about the box, that was so important to him. He'd said it was Cousin Alice's most precious possession. In that case, surely she'd have taken it with her when she went into the nursing home. Perhaps it was still there. I thought I should check that, before I went into the café. I didn't like the idea of searching through Marchant's things, even if I was looking for something that belonged here. I didn't think Marchant would like it either.

How would I find out the name of the home? Mum would probably know, Dr Lawson certainly would. I didn't see how I could ask either of them. I'd have to search in *Yellow Pages*, try the different numbers until I found the right one.

I thought about Marchant, Bo's co-pilot. Then I remembered the photo of the young men round the aeroplane, hanging in this very room. I got out of bed and switched on the light, and examined it properly for the first time. Five young men in uniform, smiling in the grim shadow of the plane – and somebody, Bo himself perhaps, had pencilled in the names underneath with the date, 1943. He wasn't there – he must have taken the picture. One person stood out from the others. He was tall and thin, and although he was smiling, he didn't look at all jolly. He had a large moustache.

I imagined him fifty years older, dressed in slacks and a hand-knitted cardigan. It was the man I'd seen in the café, I could tell without the confirmation of the faded writing underneath.

This must be the picture Bo had mentioned.

So this must have been his room. I liked the thought of that.

I went back to bed feeling much more cheerful.

Mum having a bath woke me up next morning, the rumble of the antique plumbing echoed through the house. I dressed and went down to the kitchen, wondering what I was going to do about shopping. Some onions and cereal were all we had left, and Foss was giving me a bad time because he'd run out of catfood. There was an old bike in the shed but it probably wouldn't work, and even if it did, I'd have to make two journeys. That would be the morning gone. I was worrying about this when there was a familiar bang on the door, and Dr Lawson breezed in. 'I've got a few calls in the village,' he said. 'Do you need any shopping?'

Mind reader! 'Oh we do, we need heaps of things,' I exclaimed in grateful surprise. But a voice at the back, Mum's, said, 'No, Ted, really not, we don't want to trouble you, we can manage.' He looked round and I saw how his face changed. Of course he had never seen her out of bed. She was standing filling the doorway in her long white nightgown with the ethnic shawl she uses as a dressing gown, her beautiful hair was brushed out and her blue eyes seemed huge, she should have burst into an aria. And his expression was full of admiration and yet shy at the same time, which you don't expect a doctor to be. Looking from her back to him, I saw instantly what was happening between them and I was just so glad. I couldn't be anything else, they both looked so happy.

'Florry is the housekeeper,' he said. 'It isn't any trouble, I have to go anyway. You can come too, if you like,' he added to me. 'But I don't know how long I shall be.'

I had already begun making out a list. I don't know whether he expected it to be quite so long. I put down rather nice things, and Mum gave him the money. He made her go back to bed.

But now she was on the move again, my detective work would be more complicated. How was I to conceal the phone calls I had to make? I did it by lending her my stereo, so she could listen to the tape I'd put in her stocking.

There were three places listed under Retirement Residential with the same code as ours. Acorn – not known. Weatherby House – not in our care, dear. Pastures New – Miss Vesey?

'Miss Alice Vesey.'

'Wan moment.' Rustle of pages turning. 'I'm afraid Miss Vesey passed away in March. Who is that, please?'

'Just a cousin – a distant cousin. Sorry to have bothered you. Thanks for your help.' If the lady the other end wanted more details, it was no good because I put the phone down.

Pastures New, Loampits – where was Loampits? I remembered the local map we'd used in the car, I fetched it and spread it out on the table. Loampits was about three miles south of Great Wenham. Now for the bike, to haul it out and see if I could make it go.

It was much warmer this morning, but cloudy, it looked as if it might rain. The frost had gone completely, the earth was soft, our garden had turned all green and brown. I had to shift some coal before I could reach the bike, but it seemed in working order. It needed more air in the tyres but there was a pump clipped to the frame. The brakes were rather soft, and it had no lights or gears. I wobbled down the bumpy drive, I didn't have much practice with cycling. But the tyres stayed up, so if it had a puncture it was only a slow one. I guessed Cousin Alice had used it to get about. There was no garage at the house, so she hadn't had a car. I imagined her sitting very upright, pedalling slowly. I imagined a lined face with a thin mouth, iron-grey scraped-back hair.

Mum was still listening to her new tape. I scribbled a note and left it on the kitchen table – 'Gone for bike ride, back soon, X F'. Then I set off.

The bike was heavy, and I had to push it up all the hills. Soon my legs began to ache. But it was still far quicker than walking, and the signpost to Loampits was on our side of the village so it really wasn't far. Once I turned off, the lane was all downhill, and I could freewheel. I didn't meet any traffic.

I thought I'd have to ask the way to Pastures New in the village, but it was easy to find. There was a smart white gate onto the road, with the name in black on a white board beside it. I left my bike inside the gate, and walked up the thickly gravelled drive. All was clean and neat – tight grass, clipped bushes, new paint on the double-fronted modern house. I walked up a ramp – wheelchairs – and rang the bell. I waited but nothing happened. Then I noticed the words RING AND ENTER on a card by the bell. So I entered.

The entrance hall was narrow, with stairs at the end. A desk on the left had two telephones on it, but the chair behind was empty, though a cardigan hung on the back. I waited, not knowing what to do next. Then I suddenly realised that my hands were black with coal dust – I hadn't thought of washing before I came out. Probably there was some on my face as well, and I looked about for a loo, but there wasn't one in the hall.

After a while a young nurse came down the stairs, so trim, so brisk, I was horribly conscious of my soot, my baggy jacket which had been Mum's, my unclean boots, and then my hair must have been in a startling state after the bike ride as I wasn't wearing my cap. She took me in with a cool stare and said, 'Can I help you?'

'I'm sorry to bother you – I suppose – It's about Miss Alice Vesey.'

'Are you a relation?'

'Yes, a sort of cousin – pretty distant. She left her house to my mother.'

'I see.' Nurse hooked her thumbs into the belt round her incredibly small waist and waited for me to say more.

'I suppose you didn't know her by any chance?'

'I know everyone here. I looked after Miss Vesey.'

'I was wondering – what would have happened to the things she brought with her? Like small personal things.'

I could see Nurse thought me a gold-digger. She said severely, 'She didn't bring much. Just her handbag and a few clothes. They'd have gone back to her family.'

That meant us. Suddenly I had an idea.

'Did she have any visitors?'

'Your mother never came to see her.'

'No. None of us knew each other. It's the truth. We'd never even met.'

Nurse thought about this and decided it might be a fair excuse. She said in a slightly warmer tone, 'Miss Vesey wasn't with us very long.'

'I just wondered whether anyone did visit her.'

'Her doctor.'

'Yes, of course. Was there anyone else?'

'One elderly friend. He only came once. I don't know what he was called.'

'Might he have been a tall thin man, sort of bald, with a moustache?'

'That's the one. He'll have signed the visitors' book – I can look him up.'

She took the book from the desk, and flicking back the pages to March, checked the entries. 'That's odd,' she said, frowning because the system hadn't worked. 'He never signed. Going by this, Miss Vesey had no visitors at all, apart from Dr Lawson. But I remember that man. I came into her room while he was there. He was getting a handkerchief for her out of her handbag. Why? Is there a problem?'

'No.' My cheeks were hot with excitement.

'She was almost blind, you know. Did you know that?' I shook my head. The Cousin Alice I'd imagined had sharp eyes, and a sharp tongue as well. The nurse went on, 'I was with her when she died. She was holding my hand, she thought I was her brother.'

That brought tears I couldn't stop to my eyes. She saw them and said, 'I was sorry, too. She didn't communicate much, but given time we could have been friends.'

'Thanks very much. You've been really kind,' I muttered.

'That's okay. I'm glad I came down.'

As I went down the drive, I noticed another sign marked DELIVERIES, with an arrow pointing to the back of the house. That was how Marchant had got in. No visitors' book round there.

I got my bike and glanced at my watch – it was nearly one thirty. I hustled myself through the gate and set off at full slow power. Now, of course, it was all uphill as far as Great Wenham, and soon I had to push the old bicycle. I'd skimmed down so fast I hadn't noticed the way, and when I came to a fork I hadn't a clue where to go. I opted for left and struggled on another mile, until I saw a pub and I knew I hadn't passed that. So I zoomed back to the fork. I was very anxious now. It was after two, and Mum would be worrying about me and imagining the worst.

The right-hand lane was like a tunnel between high banks with hedges along the top of them that often met in the middle. It started to rain, a thin, penetrating drizzle that dripped from the leaves as well as the sky, and soon soaked through my jacket and the legs of my jeans. Then I reached another fork. But as I stood dithering, trying to decide which way to go and feeling like screaming with frustration, who should I see but Dog, sitting in the middle of the lane on my right as if he was waiting for me. I was extremely glad to see him, even though he ignored my cry of joy. At least I had a reason for going that way, and I pushed on, and he trotted just ahead. 'Home, Dog! Home!' I shouted, encouragingly. Sure enough – after a while, the country began to look familiar. We turned into another, wider lane, and there was our house just along the road on the right.

I leapt on the bike, tore down the road, skidded into our drive, scorched to the back door. I threw down the bike on the path and flung the door open. There were two boxes of groceries on the table, and my note. I seized a chocolate bar which was sticking out of one of the boxes and went out again to share it with Dog, but he'd gone. I called him and ran to the gate and looked up and down the lane but he was nowhere to be seen. So I ate it myself. Then I went in to face Mum.

She was sitting in bed with her specs on, surrounded by sheets of manuscript paper. I was lucky – Mum when she's composing loses all sense of time, and everything else for that matter. She looked up at me, beaming, and passed me a sheet of paper. 'What do you think of that?'

I scanned it as well as I could, and said, 'It looks good.'

'Doesn't it,' she said with satisfaction. 'I really think I may have something there. Are you wet, darling?' she asked, noticing me.

'A bit. Did you read my note?'

'No. Where did you put it?'

'In the kitchen.'

'Oh, I didn't go in there. What did it say?'

'Just I went out on Cousin Alice's bike. It's a good bike.'

'Oh good.' But she wasn't really listening.

I made her a ham salad and took it up with cheese and biscuits and coffee. She might think of eating it. I was feeling agitated because of the time. It was after three already, and still raining. Soon it would start getting dark. If I cycled to the café on my lightless bike, I might have to walk back, and my torch was useless. It might be best to put it off till tomorrow. That would give me more time to work out how to get rid of Marchant while I found the box and removed it.

66

I ate a plateful of ham and tomatoes and pickled onions, while I tried to decide what to do. The sensible thing was to postpone my visit, but what if, by some appalling chance, Marchant was leaving today? In that case the box would never come back, and Bo would never be free. He would be drearily tied to this place, instead of being where he wanted to be. I longed to see him again, that was true, but not on those terms.

I heard a car in the drive, and because I'd been thinking about Marchant, I was suddenly afraid it was him. But it was only Dr Lawson. 'Wet, isn't it?' he said as he came in.

'How soon will it be dark?'

'Not for an hour or so. Why? Are you going out anywhere?'

'I thought I might just bike up to the village.'

'You've time enough for that. I hope I didn't forget anything on your list.'

'Oh no, not at all. Thanks a lot for doing all that. It would have taken me ages. How are your puppies?'

'Very nice. You must come over soon and have a look. How's your mother?'

'She's fine, she's working.' He looked surprised, and disapproving. 'She's writing music.' I thought perhaps I'd better prepare him, so I added, 'It can make her seem a bit mad. But don't worry, it doesn't mean anything.'

'I expect she'd rather not be disturbed.'

'No, I'm sure she'd like to see you. You'll find out, anyway. She never manages to hide her reactions.'

I noticed he wasn't carrying his bag, so this was a social call. Soon I heard Mum laughing upstairs. It was good for her to see someone who made her laugh.

Chapter Seven

I put on a dry sweater and an anorak and my cap, and took a pound from the change Dr Lawson had left on the table, because I thought it might be useful to have something to eat at the café, if it was open. That way I could do a bit of sussing out. Rainwater streamed off the frame of the old bike as I heaved it up, and the tyres needed more air, but that didn't take long. My legs started aching again as soon as I got on, but I pedalled strongly past Dr Lawson's battered red Ford, and turned right for Great Wenham.

The only thing I met on the road was a tractor, pulling an empty trailer. The farmer waved as he passed, so I waved back and grinned. I sang as I rode along to keep my mind off my aching legs, and although it was raining steadily I felt cheerful. I was suddenly sure that everything was going to work out all right.

I was wrong. As I came into the square, my heart skipped a beat and plunged into gloom. An estate car was parked outside the café. The boot was open, and as I watched in horror, Marchant limped out carrying a large sealed box in his arms.

Too late! the saddest words in the English language.

I watched in despair as he shoved the box into the boot. He looked older from this distance, bent and feeble. If he'd been a stranger I might even have offered to help. He spent some time pushing the box right in, so he must have only just started to load. At last he straightened, getting his breath. I thought he might have a heart problem. He shambled back into the café.

Offer to help. I shot across the square, jumped off the bike and left it up the alleyway alongside the café, out of sight in case he recognised it. I didn't want him to connect me with Cousin Alice. I was loitering casually nearby as he came out again, this time with a box of books. His expression was more disagreeable than ever. 'Do you want a hand?' I said with what I hoped was a winning smile.

'No, I don't,' he replied, very surly. But providentially several books fell off the box, so I bent down like lightning, picked them up, brushed off the puddle water with my sleeve and put them into the boot. 'Too bad you weren't loading yesterday, before it rained,' I lied.

'—rain,' he said. He seemed in a state of suppressed rage. I guessed he usually was, by the lines on his face. He didn't tell me to go away, however, so as he tried to manoeuvre the tall cardboard box, overloaded with books, into the back of the boot, I offered to get in and pull. Which I did, while he was still grumbling, and had it in place in a moment.

A big zip-up bag came out next. It was soft and bulky, I guessed it contained his clothes. I pushed it against the back seat, and while he bumbled away I quickly unzipped it and felt through the contents with both hands. No box, not even a small one. I can add that I didn't like doing this. But people shouldn't take advantage of blind old ladies.

Next came more boxes, and some plants. I didn't allow myself to be touched by the care he took of those plants. And then the boot was full, and he slammed down the lid.

'I suppose you want a cup of tea,' he said, without looking at me.

'That would be great.'

So I followed him into the café.

A swing door at the back led straight into the kitchen. He went in there to put the kettle on. He'd take at least five minutes to get out the cups and so on – There was another door, on the left. I slipped through and found myself in a narrow passage with three doors. The first led into a bathroom, the second a sitting room, empty apart from chairs, a table and TV. The last was his bedroom door, and I crept in with a thumping heart, for this was by far the most likely place. Nothing under the mattress on the bed. Nothing in the bedside cupboard. Nothing in the tacky wardrobe whose door wouldn't shut properly. And a chest of drawers – I pulled them out one after the other – nothing, nothing, nothing—

'What are you up to?' I heard a growl behind me.

I spun round, my cheeks flaming with guilt. 'I was looking for the loo.'

'What? In the chest of drawers?'

He stood aside to let me through the doorway, herded me into the café. He'd drawn the curtains across the window. Two cups of tea waited in hideous intimacy on the darkest of the little tables. We sat down together in front of them. I don't think I've ever felt so uncomfortable in my life. He stared at me with his gummy pale blue eyes.

'Haven't I seen you before?'

'I shouldn't think so.' But his old mind was grinding away. I knew he would remember.

'It was on Christmas Day, wasn't it? You came spying on me through the window. *What do you want?*'

I didn't answer. I felt fear like cold fingers

running up and down my spine. I thought he was pretty psycho.

'Aren't you the new people at Alice Vesey's place?'

'What makes you think that?'

I could see his chest heaving inside the knitted cardigan, as if he was gathering rage. He said, 'If I had a daughter who told lies like you, I'd put her across my knee.'

This made me so furious I couldn't look at him. That was when I noticed his jacket, hanging up behind the door. I hadn't finished my tea, I hadn't even started it. I got up and said, 'It's warm in here. I'm going to take off my anorak,' and I crossed the room and hung it over his. Then I went back to my seat. I drank some tea and said, 'You might thank me for the help I gave you.'

'Oh, no. I knew you were after something.' He stared at me. His face was horribly close, and there were hairs in his nose, and beads of tea on his droopy moustache. His eyes were wild and blank. No one could possibly argue against eyes like that, or make them see reason.

'You just tell whoever sent you, that there's such a thing as moral injustice, and it rankles more and more over the years,' he said. 'You tell them there's such a thing as a hero, who wasn't given a chance to prove it. There's such a thing as the wrong person getting all the glory. And there's such a thing as that hero, who nobody ever praised, striking out for himself to put things right. Until that's done, there's no rest, day or night.'

'Okay,' I said. 'I'd better go. Thanks for the tea anyway. When are you leaving?'

'Why do you want to know?'

'I don't, I was being polite.'

'You aren't polite,' he snarled. 'You're nosy. You get your long nose out of my business.' My nose isn't long, not particularly.

I went to get my anorak. He was behind me still sitting at the table. While I got it down, it was easy to feel against the pockets of his old tweed jacket underneath, for any sort of a box in them. But there wasn't. That was when the knowledge that I'd failed really hit me. I could have sat down on the floor of that horrible café and cried.

I opened the door, and saw to my dismay that it was now quite dark. I heard Marchant scrape back his chair and shuffle across the floor. I stepped out quickly into the rain. He watched me all the way to the street which led to our lane, before he went in and shut the door.

Everything was wrecked. He had the box he had stolen from poor Cousin Alice in her helplessness, and there was nothing left that I could do. As I crossed the square it wasn't only the rain that ran down my face. It was hot, hopeless tears.

Then I saw Dog sitting in the church-yard.

Dog was my friend. I climbed the wall and went in for comfort. I wanted to sit beside him under the yew tree, put my arm round him, tell him how miserable everything was. But as I approached, he got up and trotted off among the graves. I stopped, and called out, 'Dog!' in a dismal voice. Surely he could understand how desperately unhappy I was.

He turned and sat, waiting for me. 'Please, Dog, come!' I said.

Still he waited. When I went towards him, he got up and trotted on. There were no lamps in the churchyard, but those in the square and people's houses meant that I could see, more or less. The uncut grass was soaking now, the graves spooky tumbledown shapes, the yew trees like mourners in cloaks. Soon I saw the outline of the solitary cross – REMEMBERED WITH PRIDE.

Dog was on the grave again, frantically scrabbling. I ran up to him. I saw at once that though the earth had thawed, he still wasn't making any holes.

Suddenly I understood. I knelt down on that wet grave and pulled at the turf. A square chunk came up easily – it had been cut through. Dog sat close by, watching me.

I clawed, I dug. I could see across the square to the café, and the light was still on. I dug for many desperate minutes before I felt the corner of a box. I raised my head and saw Marchant open the door and come out. I hoped he was going to put something into the car, but no, he was crossing the square.

My heart was beating very fast. I lifted out the muddy box, which was quite small and light, and put it into my anorak pocket. Dog was still watching, motionless. Then – he simply wasn't there any more.

I pushed back the earth and stamped it down just as Marchant came through the gate. I dashed to where the gravestones stood thickest, I was hardly in their shelter before he reached the cross. He started digging, with a trowel from the noise. Suddenly he turned on a torch. Bo's cross shone incandescent in the brilliant beam. If I'd been him and seen it like that, I'd have given up in fear and shame. But all he did was switch off and start digging again. He dug on for several minutes. He couldn't believe that box had gone. When he found out, I knew he'd know I'd taken it. He'd come straight after me.

I was ducking and dodging from grave to grave, heading for the square. There was no point in getting the bike – without any lights I'd crash as soon as I left the village. I'd have gone across country if I'd known the way, but the thought of being lost in a field that might have a bull in it was even worse than Marchant. My heart was pounding so hard, I didn't notice when the trowel stopped scraping, but next instant a brilliant ray of light swept the churchyard. I froze. He switched off, waited in case I moved. I didn't. He switched on again, made another careful search with that frighteningly powerful torch. If he'd gone in among the graves, he couldn't have missed me. Instead he went to the end wall and leaned over and played the light along it, and after that he scanned the field below the wood – by which time I was safely into the square. My legs had been aching badly all afternoon, but now I ran like a hare. I knew he could hear me in my boots, but I also knew that I could run a lot faster than he could.

In a city there are always people about, but Great Wenham was empty. Everyone was inside, eating supper or watching TV. The sound of my own feet thudding down the deserted street was horribly scary. Maybe Marchant would know a short-cut, jump out in front of me. My breath was sobbing out and I had a crippling stitch in my side.

Soon I was clear of the village. Two dark miles of lane lay ahead between me and home, but there had to be time to stop, just to get my breath. But as I stood gasping on the verge, I heard the furious revving of an engine in the square, and instantly I remembered two things. Marchant had a car, and he knew where I lived.

I looked round desperately for somewhere to hide. There wasn't a gateway. No way could I creep into the hedge – I tried, but it was much too thick. There were no trees near enough to climb, and if I went back to the village for help, I'd run straight into him. I was trapped.

The glare of his headlights was speeding towards me. He was driving fast in low gear, the way people do when they're furious. He'd be with me in just a few seconds. I couldn't move. My throat ached with unscreamed screams. I waited for him like a dummy.

Then I was suddenly bathed in light from the opposite direction. I whirled round. Another car was approaching. It slowed, stopped, the door was flung open, Dr Lawson leant out. 'Florence!' he exclaimed. 'What on earth are you doing out here?'

It was like the end of a nightmare. Behind me, Marchant slammed on his brakes. 'Well, hop in,' said the doctor. 'Here's somebody wanting to pass.'

I scrambled in with my knees buckling. It was lucky that Dr Lawson was concentrating on the other car or he would have asked me what was wrong. The lane was so narrow, Marchant could only just squeeze past. I had plenty of time to study his face, caught in the beam of our headlights, but I only gave it a glance. It was a mask of rage and hate, and his hands gripped the wheel as if he wanted to throttle it. I hope I never again see anyone who looks like that.

'Sick-looking bloke,' said the doctor, viewing him with a professional eye. 'He's only been here a year, he kept the tea shop in the village. People stopped going in there. It's a good thing he's leaving.'

On the way home, Dr Lawson lectured me about how the country could be just as dangerous as the town for a young girl at night. (I had already found this out.) It was certainly sensible not to try to ride a bike without lights, but it would have been even more sensible to ring Mum from Great Wenham.

I sat listening, I didn't say anything. I was holding onto the box in my anorak pocket.

'Is Mum in a state?' I asked when he'd finished.

'Not too much. I told her I knew where you were, and I said I'd fetch you.'

'Thanks a lot.'

He gave me a quick smile. 'That's okay.'

He said no more about it, and he has never mentioned it since. I do like him very much.

When we got home I went straight upstairs to my room and put the box under my pillow. I didn't want to open it yet. It was only a small black box, and it would have to contain something pretty special, to be worth all the pain and grief.

Chapter Eight

No matter how much you love your parents, no matter how well you get on together, you soon learn that there are certain things they don't understand. Mum's always afraid that I'm nervous and over-imaginative, because that's the way *she* is. I knew that if I told her about Bo, she'd get frantically worried, because obviously she'd believe it had all happened in my head and I must be deeply unhappy about something (probably Dad). I didn't want any of that.

I went into her bedroom. She was sitting up in bed with Foss extended, purring, beside her. There was an old brown handbag open on her knees, which I had never seen before. She looked up at me and took off her specs and said, 'Oh darling love, *what* have you been doing all this time?'

'I just biked to the village. I went into the churchyard – I was in there for a bit—'

'Why the *churchyard*?'

'Well there isn't a lot to do in Great Wenham, is there? Oh, and I had some tea in the café – I'm really sorry it got so late. I didn't mean to worry you—'

'No, no, it was all right because Ted went out to look for you. It was lucky he was still here. Otherwise I would have come out after you myself. Anyway I'm allowed to get up properly tomorrow, so we'll be able to do things together. You must have been very lonely and bored.'

'No, honestly – What have you got there?'

'Oh, this is old Cousin Alice's handbag. The solicitors sent it to me with her other bits and pieces. I meant to sort through it ages ago and I forgot. But Florry, look what I've found.' She handed me a sheet of paper. 'Read it.' She watched my face as I read. 'Pretty splendid, isn't it?'

'Yes.' It was all I could do to bring out that one word.

'It's what you call a citation. You see he won the D.F.C.'

'There's a cross to him in the church-yard.'

'I expect it's a memorial cross. I don't imagine they ever found his body, poor boy. And look here—' again she rummaged in the bag. 'A picture.'

The snapshot was faded, but there stood Bo, exactly as I knew him. He had his arm round the shoulders of a smiling girl with dark curly hair. They were standing on the step outside the french windows. The sun was shining on them, making white patches on the old photograph, the flowers were out. A spaniel I knew well sat at their feet. On the back, Alice had written, *Pilot officer Beau and me and Bungy. 9 May 1943'*

'I expect that was taken when he got his commission. It makes you feel proud, doesn't it? To be related to someone like that.'

I couldn't talk at all about how I felt. I said, 'Can I keep it?'

'Of course.'

After a while I said, 'You know Dr Lawson said he'd give me a puppy.'

'Did he? I thought you wanted to go back to London. We can't have a puppy in the flat.'

'I don't want to go back to the flat. I want to stay here. Then I can have a puppy. I shall call him Bungy.'

Pilot Officer Beaumont Vesey was coming home after an anti-submarine raid in the Bay of Biscay. The plane had been hit, and a fire started. All the way they struggled to put it out, but by the time they reached the North Devon coast, he knew that he couldn't land. He ordered the crew to bale out, and himself flew on in the blazing aircraft which exploded over the Bristol Channel before he could escape.

'Pilot Officer Vesey has at all times displayed great skill, sound judgement and reliability.'

I stood by my bed in Bo's room, that was my room now, remembering the dream I'd had the night we came here. His citation was that dream in writing.

I folded the paper and put it under my pillow, and took out the box. It was earthy,

I wiped it clean. The letters DFC appeared, stamped in gold on the lid.

An elaborate silver cross lay in the box. In the centre was a circle with a crown at the top, and the letters RAF in the middle. The circle had a laurel wreath round it. Two feathery wings stretched out from it on each side, along the arms of the cross. It hung on a piece of thick ribbon with diagonal stripes of violet and white.

I was looking at Bo's Distinguished Flying Cross. He hadn't seen it – he never would see it, because it had been awarded after he died.

I took it out of the box and carried it to the window. The rain had stopped, but there were no stars. The night was black dark and still. I opened the window as wide as I could and leaned out over the garden. We were going to have a beautiful garden here. I couldn't imagine living anywhere else.

The cross had warmed to the temperature of my hand. It was like holding his heart. I knew he knew it was back. I knew I wouldn't see him again.

Then the black sky began to throb, faintly

at first, but the noise grew louder and louder. I guessed it was a low-flying aircraft, different from the ones I was used to. As it approached I could hear the regular thud of the engines, like the giant heartbeat of a storm. I thought it must be very low indeed. It sounded as though it would take our roof off.

The door opened and Mum came in, and joined me at the window. 'My God, something's flying low,' she said, and we stared in the direction the roar was coming from. Soon we saw the shape of it, dark on dark. 'No lights!' she said. 'My *God*, imagine flying this low with no lights on a night like this. They must be crazy!' For the plane was following the contour of the hill, it was over the fields, over the lane, over our garden where the tallest of the trees seemed to be reaching out to touch it as it went by. The noise was deafening. I felt Mum flinch and I know she ducked, but I stood straight and tall by the open window. It passed – and then it wheeled and soared up into the sky, and in a moment it had gone, and there was silence.

Goodbye, Bo. Goodbye. But this time I didn't have that terrible feeling of loss. It was simply like a line ruled underneath. The End.

Mum said, 'If it wasn't utterly ridiculous, I'd say the mad pilot in that plane was putting on a show for us.'

I said, 'If Doctor could see you standing by the open window without your shawl, *he* would be mad.'

'You like him, don't you?'

'Yes. I like him a lot.'

'So do I.' She looked at me and said, 'I'm getting very fond of him, Florry. Do you mind?'

'Not at all. I'm glad.'

She put her arm round me and kissed me. Then I opened my hand and showed her the cross. She took it and looked at it carefully under the light. She was moved, I could see.

'Where did you find this?' she asked after a while.

'I will tell you. But if you don't mind, I'll write it all down. It would make it easier for you to understand.'

So that's what I did.